STALK ME NOW

FRANKIE LOVE

COPYRIGHT

Cover Design by Cormar Covers

STALK ME NOW

When offered a housesitting job at a Malibu
mansion, I leap at the chance.
A view of the ocean and a quiet place to paint
means my last summer before finishing art
school might be my best one yet.
But things change the moment I arrive.
Someone's watching me.
I should be scared.
Instead, I'm turned on.
Someone is lurking the shadows and it's making
me bold in ways I've never been before.
Maybe it's not a creative outlet I need... maybe it's
a sexual one.

Dear Reader,

This is short, steamy, and will get your summer started with a bang!

Xo, Frankie

1

———————

OLIVIA

I am so freaking horny!

I spent the last few months in a cramped apartment listening to my three roommates have boink-fests with their boyfriends and it has made me dizzy with desire. Considering I am way too picky (and not at all attracted to college boys – I prefer real men, thank you very much), I am single as ever and my poor pussy is pissed.

Still, this housesitting gig is the respite I need. I can't concentrate in that apartment with all the shenanigans, and I have *got* to finish some paintings if I want my senior portfolio ready when classes resume at my art college this fall.

As I pull my car outside the malibu mansion where I will be crashing for a few months, I know that I made the right choice in coming out here today.

When my mom's old friend Leanne posted on her social media about needing someone to come and look after her home while she was on vacation, I swear, I responded so fast she must have thought that I was stalking her. There was no way that I was going to let anyone else get their hands on this place. No, it's mine! And I'm going to revel in the opportunity to have some space away from my roommates and my real life, even if I know it won't last forever.

Honestly, it's not that I don't like my roommates. They're pretty good, as roommates go, but sometimes it just gets a little too hard for me to wrap my head around sharing my space with other people. Especially not when I need to clear my head to get my painting done.

It's been nearly impossible to work on my stuff with Tara, Leila, and Paula around all the time – not to mention their boyfriends coming in and out like they own the place too. I'm glad that they've all fallen in love, but I just wish it was a slightly less loud, more roommate-respectful kind of love, you know? When I'm trying to work on my art in my bedroom and all I can hear is them freakishly fooling around next door, the creative juices are hardly flowing the way they used to.

But now I'm going to be spending the summer looking after Leanne's gorgeous mansion in Malibu, and I am going to make the very most of it. I step out of my old beat-up second-hand car, and grab my stuff from the back seat. Aside from my bag of clothes, there's not much I'm bringing, just an easel and some paints, as well as a cloth for the floor to make sure that I don't leave a single stain behind at Leanne's gorgeous place. A free place to live with incredible views and a spectacular amount of space – there is no way I am ruining this opportunity.

The summer air is bright and crisp, and it kind of feels as though the universe is telling me that I am doing something right here. Not that I have ever been much of a believer in the universe, but if I was, I would feel it right now. I suppose that makes me an anomaly in the art world, since all the kids I went to college with seemed to be caught up in the idea of the wind whispering things to them and the sound of the raindrops on windows tapping out Morse code as to what they should paint next, or something. I mean, if it works for them, great, but I've always had other things in mind.

I fumble in my pocket for the key that Leanne gave me, and, as I unlock the heavy front gate, I can't fight the feeling that someone is watching me right now.

I glance around to try and figure out where that feeling's coming from, but I can't locate anything that might tip me off. Huh. Strange. Chalking it up to being in an unfamiliar place, I close the gate behind me and walk along the path to the house.

As I push the door open, I take in the foyer, the massive ceilings, everything white – and everything *so* quiet. This place is so peaceful. I can't remember the last time that I actually had this sort of stillness around me that didn't involve me putting in noise-cancelling headphones and wedging the door to the bathroom shut. But I don't want to focus on the negative. I want to zoom in on the fact I am here now, and that is all that matters.

I head straight up to the office, which looks out over this absurdly beautiful garden outside, and throw open the windows. This is where I'm going to paint, I've decided. I can see across the garden, into the house next door and the one down the street from me, too. I don't know how Leanne fills this space all by herself, compared to my cramped apartment, it feels like a palace.

I wander up to the guest bedroom, wanting to see where I will be sleeping this summer. Leanne told me via text that it was the second master. I had no idea homes had two master suites, but I will take this massive king-size bed, walk-in closet, and double-head shower. I take a photo of the bathroom and text my mother.

Me: Thanks again for telling Leanne I was trustworthy. This place is amazing!

Mom: Great honey. Now you can focus on your painting. I believe in you.

Smiling, I tuck the phone in the back pocket of my cutoff jean shorts, and make a last visit to the car to make sure that I've got everything and that it's locked up, humming a little tune to myself as I go. I drop my bag of clothes as I stumble over my bare feet on the concrete drive, but quickly scoop it back up, laughing at my clumsiness. Nothing is going to sour my mood today.

I can't remember the last time that I felt this happy, felt this alive, felt as though everything was falling into place for me. I can't wait to see the stuff I create while I'm here; I've had a few ideas of pieces I want to work on, but I haven't had the mental —or physical – space to tease them out.

I rummage through the drawers in the enormous, open-plan kitchen looking for a takeout menu – turns out that Leanne doesn't keep any around. Probably because she has a live-in chef here most of the time, anyway. I pull out my phone and locate a local Vietnamese place that looks good to me. I'm looking forward to having the chance to cook in here, but right now, I want to veg out on the couch with some noodles and revel in the quiet around me.

I glance out of the window once I've put in my order, wondering how I am going to see the delivery driver arrive from all the way out here – but instead of the food, I find myself focused on the man who has just emerged from a car at the bottom of the driveway next door. He glances over to my car in surprise, and grins to himself as he heads to the house. I wish I was outside, so we could meet, but I'm not going to run out there now like a weirdo. His salt-and-pepper hair and knowing eyes tell me he has plenty of experience in life. He's tall, broad shouldered, wearing work-out clothes and carrying a water bottle.

He's sexy. Really sexy, actually. The kind of sexy that gets under your skin and inside your head even when you know it's not meant to. He's got hair cropped short to show off his angular features, strong jaw, steady eyes. I sink my teeth into my bottom lip as I watch the neighbor heading up the driveway, pulling open his front door.

And I know that this summer has just gotten a hell of a lot more interesting.

2

GAGE

As I WALK to my mail box, I can't stop staring at the lime green bikini top that is next to the passenger door. Dropped or forgotten. I want to walk over and grab it, but it's not my property.

Still. That triangle top has me curious.

Beyond that, nobody around here drives a beat-up car like that. Even the workers who come by to do gardens and mechanical shit don't – they have big trucks. Anyone who's turning up in a vehicle like that one clearly hasn't spent a lot of time in neighborhoods like this. And I have to admit, there's a part of me that's intrigued to find out what else is going on here.

Leanne is away for a while, though I'm not sure to where – I guess she's got someone to keep an eye on the house for her while she's out of town. But who? And the lime green bikini top must belong to the owner of whoever is staying there. That is a hell of an intriguing prospect to me right now.

I pour myself a drink in the kitchen and keep my eyes pinned on the car outside, waiting for whoever owns it to come out again – and sure enough, it doesn't take long till she shows her face.

It's a woman, quite a lot younger than me. She has blonde hair and eyes so blue that I can see them from all the way over here. She's wearing a cropped tee and some high waisted tight and tiny jean shorts, hair pulled back into a messy ponytail at the top of her head, barefoot as she comes down the path, a pair of glasses tucked into the V of her shirt. My eyes linger on her big tits, bouncing as she walks.

Hmm. Even more interesting. I take another sip of my drink, and thank God that I decided to come back from that business trip a day early. Nate, the co-owner of my company, tried to convince me to stick it out at the conference a little longer, but honestly, something had been pulling me home. And now I can see exactly what it was.

I head back out to my car to find some papers – or at least, that's what I'll tell her if she's still out there. Is she in that house all by herself? Big place to fill with just her presence, though maybe that's what she likes about it. I watch as she notices the swimsuit top on the driveway next to her car. She bends over, grabs for it, and balls it up in her hand. My eyes linger on her curvy little ass when she bends down though, giving me idea son how I'd like to bend her across my bed.

Damn. I need to cool down. But she is so damn sexy it's impossible not to imagine her with me.

A guy pulls up on a moped and she hands him a generous tip before she grabs the bag that he is carrying. Before she can vanish inside, I take a step forward. No way I'm going to miss out on introducing myself to my new neighbor.

"Hey," I greet her, and she glances up at me. Close up, I can see some freckles on her face, and I have to admit, she's even cuter than I thought. She smiles at me, lighting her whole face up at once.

"Oh, hi!" she exclaims. "You must be my new neighbor..."

"Yeah, I must be," I reply. "I'm Gage. And you are...?"

"Olivia," she replies, and she extends her hand to me, balancing the stuff that she is carrying against her hip as she does so. "Nice to meet you. I'm looking after this house while Leanne's out of town."

"Whole place all to yourself, huh?" I remark, and she nods.

"That's the plan," she agrees. "I can't wait. I live in the city with my roommates normally. I think I'm going to get addicted to having all this space to myself."

"Well, if you ever need any company, let me know," I reply, and she rests her teeth on her bottom lip for a moment.

"I'll be sure to." She tucks a loose strand of her light hair back behind her ear. "Uh, and thanks for the welcome to the neighborhood. I know I probably stick out like a sore thumb here."

"Well, got to admit, I haven't seen a car like yours in a while," I reply, gesturing to the run-down vehicle beside us. She bursts out laughing.

"I didn't even think about that," she laughs. "Yeah, I guess I'm not exactly making myself easy to ignore, right?"

"Guess you're not," I reply, and I let my eyes linger on hers for just a moment too long. She pauses, parts her lips as though there is something else that she wants to say to me, but instead, she just nods again.

"Good to meet you," she repeats herself, and I

notice a little pink tinge to her cheeks as she hustles back up the driveway with her food in her hands. I watch her as she goes, and I can't help but smile. See? There's always a good reason to come back home.

Especially when there's someone as cute as her waiting for me right next door.

3

OLIVIA

THE COOL AIR whips in from the ocean not far from here, and I smile as I set up my easel on the back porch. I planned to work from the study, but I can't resist the saltwater-tinged air.

The temperature is perfect out here, a perfect chance for me to do a little warm-up work before I get down to my real plans. I tip my head back and let it flow through me, the sweet comfort of knowing that I don't have to worry about getting under anyone's feet when I go to the bathroom later. Is there anything better than this? If there is, I haven't found it yet, and I don't want to, either.

Anyway. I set up my paints on a stool beside my easel and look down over the flush of flowers in front of me. Leanne has the most gorgeous garden, and I feel like I have been blessed with a trip to the Palace of Versailles or something getting to paint here; there are a line of pink peonies, their buds parted, like lips trying to speak something into the wind.

I push the robe that I'm wearing off my shoulders, and perch on the stool that I have set up to work from. I'm wearing shorts and a sports bra; after my morning workout I didn't feel like changing. Besides, calling it a workout is a bit of a stretch considering I kept pausing the YouTube video while the instructor was telling me to do sit-ups to take bites of the donut and sips of the coffee I had delivered this morning.

What can I say, I prefer carbs over aerobics.

In my shorts and top, I am fully covered, enough to make sure that I don't flash anything too intense to the neighbors. Not that I would exactly mind the one neighbor I met seeing a little more of me. Gage, that's his name – and gosh, he's even hotter close-up than I had been ready for. Last night I made up an entire fantasy that he had come outside to introduce himself as a way to flirt with me, and the little scenario helped me fall asleep. I like the idea that a sexy older man would find me attractive.

I am sure it is all in my head, but there was something about the way that he looked at me, the way that he offered me a little company if I wanted it, that makes it hard to think straight.

I glance to his house next door and feel a little flicker of excitement rush through me. So what if he can see me? I wouldn't mind at all. If I'm going to be here all summer long then I want to make it a memorable one, that's for sure.

I slip the shorts down my body and kick them off so that I am in nothing but my sports bra and panties. Plausible deniability, I can just say that I was getting too warm and needed to cool off. Besides, it's basically a swimsuit, right?

I pick up my paintbrush and dip it into the red, mix it with a little white on my palette, and then lift it to the easel so I can start making some strokes.

There is something about the sensuality of the cool air on my skin that thrills me. I am not sure what it is, but I am certain that I can feel eyes on me, feel myself being watched. It doesn't bother me, though. In fact, there is something in it that I enjoy – the cool air on my skin is balanced by the heat of those eyes on me, whether or not they are actually real.

I become absorbed in the painting that is coming to life, bringing the peonies romantic in their soft, pastel-pink sweetness. They remind me of summer back where I grew up in Northern

California, the heat of the sun beating down on me. I mix the pink till it's perfect, until I know that nothing else would capture them better, and mark out soft shapes on the easel before me.

It doesn't take long before even the sports bra that I'm wearing starts to feel like more than I need right now. I glance around again, at least pretending that I care if someone is watching me, and then pull it off over my head. I want to lure the neighbor Gage out of his house ... I want him to stalk me. Now. Though I am sure it's just me obsessing about him.

The feeling of the air against my nipples makes them harden at once. I bite my lip. I can't believe that I am actually doing this. And I can't believe just how much I am enjoying it, too.

I continue to paint, let myself get caught up in it, but this time, I am certain that I can feel someone watching me. Certain that there is someone out there, someone beyond my field of vision, who can see me. Who is enjoying everything that they see.

I never thought of myself as much of an exhibitionist, but maybe I've just been holding myself back from what I really enjoy. I run my fingers through my hair, marking a spot on my cheek with light pink paint, and take a step back from the easel. To anyone who might be looking at me right now, it would seem like a casual gesture, not one intended to mean anything to anyone. But I want to make sure that they can see me, that whoever is watching me right now can make out every inch of me.

The thought of it thrills me in ways that I can't even put into words – my pussy is throbbing at the thought of being watched, being seen, being taken in by someone else.

Slowly, I sink back down onto the stool. My thin panties are the only thing between me and the seat and I find myself grinding against it without even thinking. I don't even realize how turned on I am until I start to move my hips back and forth against this stool, needing to feel the pressure of it against my pussy.

I know that whoever is watching me – wherever they are – they must be able to tell what I am doing right now, but it's not enough to stop me. I slide my hand down between my legs, massage myself over my panties, and feel the throbbing need spread out over my whole body.

Fuck, that feels so good – I can't remember the last time I touched myself without having to worry about someone walking in on me. And yet, here I am, doing it right out in the open, where I am almost hoping that someone will look around and see me grinding against my own hand in the middle of the warm summer day.

I slip my hand beneath my panties, close my eyes, tip my head back, and let the pleasure rush through me. My pussy is so wet and so swollen that the merest touch is enough to get me moaning; I can't help it, don't want to hold back, just want to give myself over to this, the way that it feels, everything about it.

I lift my hips and push them hungrily against my fingers, using my hand as a toy to fuck myself, slipping my fingers further down and grazing the very edge of my slit before I push them inside.

"Fuck," I gasp. How long has it been since I was last fucked? I don't even remember, but I don't care. I just want to let myself loose right now. I slide my fingers in and out, in and out, fucking myself with my hand, taking my time as I bring myself nearer and nearer to the edge that I am craving so much...

And it's with that feeling, that sureness of eyes on me, that I finally fall helplessly over the edge. I cry out, loud enough that I am sure everyone in the entire neighborhood can hear me, but I don't care.

There is only one person I really want to hear me – and if he is as close as I feel like he is, then I know that he hasn't been able to miss it.

4

GAGE

I HEAR the sound of it before anything else. And I know at once that what I am hearing is everything that I have been fantasizing about since the moment that I laid eyes on Olivia.

I lift my head from the seat and look into the garden next door. I have been doing everything that I can to keep myself from staring at the woman who I know is over there, even though I have cancelled the plans for the rest of my weekend just in case she should feel so inclined as to take me up on the offer for some company.

But when I see what she is doing – when I see her, on that porch, her hand shoved down her panties, her tits bouncing as she fingers herself raw, her body mostly unclothed, barely obscured by the small easel in front of her, my jaw drops.

Okay, so I knew that she was hot before, but the sight of her like that? It's enough to make me want to vault the fence and take her on the spot.

Does she know that I can see her right now? I don't take my eyes off her. Maybe she thinks the porch is totally private. Surely, she must be aware that anyone can look over there, right? I want to call out to her, but I don't want this to be over yet. Her body is small, lean, her thighs clamping around her hand as she touches herself. I can see her swollen pink nipples from here, and I want nothing more than to just go over there and pull one into my mouth, see how she would react. Suck it until she is begging me for my cock, tease her areola until she's climbing into my lap with a wet and juicy pussy.

I draw my gaze away from her. She doesn't even know that I am watching her right now. What the hell do I think I'm doing? I can't just sit here and stare like some sort of creep. But I want to stalk her. Now.

She's in a private space, not doing this for anyone but herself. But then, why would she come outside to play with herself?

I know that there is something off here, something that I can't quite wrap my head around, but for the life of me, I can't figure out what it is. Maybe because I am so intently focused on the way she looks as that orgasm moves through her, her entire body trembling as she comes around her own hand. She looks well-practiced at that, and I wonder how she would look on top of my dick instead, that same look of helpless relief on her face as she rides me like I am the only thing on Earth that matters.

I rise to my feet. I feel as though my eyes are screaming at me, telling me to look over and take her in one more time, but I am not going to creep on her like that. As tempting as it is.

I steal one more glance before I make it inside. I don't know how I am meant to deny myself that. And God, the sight of her is enough to nearly drive me insane – does she have any idea how good she looks right now? That small, supple body of hers grinding against her hand, her head thrown back and her lips parted, just the same way that they had been before, when she was looking at me. I know that she must be feeling everything that she has ever wanted to right now, and I wish more than anything that it was my hand thrust down her panties, massaging that sweet little clit of hers, while she begs me for more, more, more.

I manage to make it inside, and close the door behind me. I need a cold shower. Several cold showers. I am not going to make her uncomfortable while she is living here. I am not going to obsess over her, no matter how tempting it might be to do just that. And I am sure as hell not going to let the sight of one naked woman drive me so crazy. Just because she's hot, just because she's close, it doesn't mean that I have to do anything about it, right?

That's what I tell myself as I step into the shower, turn it on full blast, and let the freezing-cold water rush over my skin. I don't have to do anything about it.

Even if all I want right now is to push my tongue between her lips and feel her come all over my cock.

5

OLIVIA

I FISH the last of the takeout from the fridge and throw it in the oven to warm it up. God, it's so tempting to just – to just curl up in bed with a vibrator and forget that there is anything else that I'm meant to be doing here. Am I allowed to? I know that I have been naughty, but damn, it feels so good to let off some steam for a change.

I came inside from my little painting-and-playing session to get something to eat, but I would be lying if I said that it isn't still on my mind. I can't remember the last time that I did anything as filthy as that in my life.

But there is something about the older man right next door that makes it hard to think straight. I just like the thought of him watching me so much, the thought of him seeing me in all the ways he wants to. I know from the way that he smiled at me when we first met that there is something like that on his mind, and gosh, it's so tempting to give in, call him round here and tell him that he can do anything he wants to me.

I eat a little food, but honestly, it's not the takeout that I'm hungry for. It's only my second day here, and I am already distracted from my work again. When am I going to get my shit together? I'm trying to stay focused, but instead, I can't get my mind off the man next door.

And oh, is he a *man.* I've never been with someone that much older than me before, but the thought of it excites me so much – I bet he's done things that I've never even dreamt of, and I love the idea of learning from him, having him teach me all the ways that I could be doing this better.

Maybe I should call him up. No – what if it doesn't work out and I'm stuck living next door to him for the next few months in total awkwardness? I'm not going to mess up the time I have here but getting obsessed with some guy I have only just laid eyes on.

But I am sure that he was watching me when I was out there touching myself. I could almost feel the intensity of his eyes on me and I liked it –

craved it, wished that it had been his hand down my panties instead of mine.

It's all this freedom from my roommates that's doing this to me. All this time alone, and suddenly this new version of myself is out to play again. And aimed squarely at the guy living next door. The one who can't seem to keep his eyes off of me...

As I clean up the food, I hear a noise outside – a rumble of thunder, the pitter-patter of some rain. Shit! I left my painting stuff out there, I need to grab it before it gets ruined.

I hustle my ass outside and grab the easel and the paints. A few heavy drops of rain have already smeared some of the paint I carefully laid down a couple of hours ago, and I grimace as I get it inside. Well, at least this isn't one of the ones that I care about.

I am about to grab the stool, too, when a big gust of winds hits me from the side. Shit! I stumble and drop the stool, careering towards the edge of the porch and thumping against the siderail painfully. I try to catch my footing but it's too late, and before I can stop myself, I go tumbling over the edge.

And right into the arms of the man that I haven't been able to stop thinking about since the moment that I arrived here.

6

GAGE

"Shit!" I exclaim, as I grab her before she hits the ground. Olivia grabs hold of me tight, letting out a squeal of shock.

"Are you okay?" I ask her. I knew that there was something I had come here for – something that told me I needed to do something, needed to help her before something bad happened. When I spotted the storm brewing, I knew that I needed to come over and make sure that she brought her stuff inside. When she hadn't answered the door, I had come out to the back where I had last seen her, and sure enough, she was out here – and about an inch away from losing her footing.

"Oh my God," she gasps, and she grips my arms tightly. She is trembling slightly, hanging on to me for dear life.

"Olivia, you okay?" I ask as I slowly put her back on her feet. Holding her like this, even though I know I am just doing it to help her, is way too intimate for my liking. The smell of her – vanilla mixed with paint – floods my senses, and I do my very best to ignore it.

"Yeah, I'm fine, better now, actually," she replies looking into my eyes. She tucks a loose strand of hair back behind her ear. She looks a little shaky, but she finally lets go of my shoulders.

"What are you doing here, anyway?" she asks, crossing her arms, trying to ignore the few drops of rain that are landing on her face and in her hair.

"I wanted to warn you about the storm," I reply, and she cocks her head at me.

"But how did you know that I would be out here?"

I know what she is doing, that she is trying to test me. And there is no way that I am going to fail her test right now.

"I saw you out here earlier," I reply, meeting her gaze steadily. I see that little pink tinge to her cheeks again, so endearing and so cute that it takes all that I have not to reach out and grab her and pull her close to me right here and now. But instead, she just nods.

"Hmm," she murmurs, and she glances back inside the house. "Well, can't have you going back to your place in this weather. Want to come in?"

"I'd love to," I reply, and she grabs my hand and leads me inside.

My head spins. She must have known that I was watching her. Does that mean that she put on that show earlier especially for me? Was she thinking of me when she was grinding on her hand like that?

"Thanks for coming over," she tells me as she heads to the kitchen; I follow her. I've been inside Leanne's house a couple of times before, but never with someone like this, and I've never been so distracted as I am by the sight of the woman in front of me.

"Guess you saved my ass," she continues, and she reaches into the fridge and grabs a bottle of white wine. She pours us each a glass, then hands one to me before taking a sip of her own.

"What were you doing out there, anyway?" I ask, taking a drink, my eyes on her. The way her lips glide over the top of the wine glass is making it hard to think straight.

"What are you, my stalker?" she teases me lightly. "I was bringing my easel in so the painting I was working on didn't get ruined."

I'm not much of a white wine drinker, but I

feel like she could ask me to do anything that she wants right now and I would be helpless to resist. I'm not usually the guy who gets taken in by a pretty face, but when the face happens to be as beautiful as this one, how can I resist the pull?

"You paint?" I ask as we head through to the living room. She nods to the easel that she was working on outside.

"Allegedly," she jokes. "This is the one I was doing out there."

"It's gorgeous," I remark, and she cocks an eyebrow at me.

"You think?"

It's the start of a picture of the peonies in the back yard, the ones that have just come into bloom, but honestly, the way that she has painted them – they look more like the lips of a pussy spreading. I can feel my cock ache, something electrifying passing through me, something over-heating inside of me.

"I still have some more work to do on it," she continues, her eyes tracing mine for the briefest moment. "But I think it's a good place to start. Don't you?"

"Mmm," I murmur back. "And do you always paint like this? Things that are so... explicit?"

She pauses for a moment, and I know that I have caught her off-guard. She doesn't see her painting like that, but it doesn't take long for her to tilt her head to the side and see what I see. A smile curls up the corners of her lips.

"Yes, that's where a lot of my focus lies," she replies. "I normally prefer more... body work, though."

"And do you work from models?" I ask. "Or is it just... your imagination?"

"I can go either way," she replies. "But I think it's far more realistic to work from life models. And more interesting, too."

She takes another sip of her wine, and leans on the mantel over the ornate fireplace in front of her. I know that she knows that I know what she was doing out there, when I saw her before.

The question is, should I do something about it?

I want to grab her, press my mouth against her ear and tell her that I saw what she was doing out there and that I can make her come way better than that, but I get the feeling that I need to play this slow if I am going to play it right.

"I bet someone like you has portraits of their family all over their house," she teases me.

"What's that supposed to mean?" I protest, laughing.

"You must come from money, right?" she asks,

tipping her head to the side. "To live in a place like that."

"I made it all myself," I reply, and she parts her lips, smiles.

"Impressive," she remarks. "So, what? Just pictures of you in there?"

"Are you asking if I'm single? Because I am. And the paintings in the house? There are none. I haven't gotten around to commissioning any yet," I reply. "Haven't found an artist that matches the style that I'm going for."

"And what style is that, exactly?"

"Yours," I shoot back.

She grins. I know that her mind is just where mine is right now, that the two of us are in the same place, just trying to find our way to each other.

"Well, I'd have to take some careful measurements," she purrs. She's in full sex kitten mode now, and she seems to be enjoying every second of it.

I am, too – there is something so damn hot about the way she looks at me, the confidence with which she moves through this space, as though it belongs to her.

"And how would we go about that?" I ask as she puts her beer down. She is standing so close to me now that I can smell the vanilla perfume wafting off of her skin, and I want to gorge myself on it on the spot.

"I think I would start here," she murmurs, and she reaches out and slides her hand over my pants, pressing her palm against my cock – it's already half-hard by the time that touches it, and her fingers' caress over it is enough to bring me to a rock-solid erection. I groan, and she moves a little closer to me, pressing that body of hers up against mine. I slide my hands down her waist, to her hips, and watch as she bites her lip and gazes up at me.

"Mind if I get a closer look?" she breathes, her mouth so close to mine that I can feel the words as well as hear them. I tuck my hand behind her head, and bring her in close for a kiss before she can slip away once more – and as soon as our mouths meet, everything that I have been trying to push down and ignore rises up inside of me for good.

I push my tongue into her mouth, kissing her hard, her body moving against mine as though I am the most delicious thing in the world. I tighten my grip on the back of her neck, pull her in close, and let my teeth catch on her lip for the barest moment as she rubs her hand over my package.

"Mmm," she moans playfully, and she pulls

back to look into my eyes, a playful expression on her face. And I know, at once, that I don't stand a chance against this girl. There is nothing I can do to hide how into her I am. And I don't want to pretend for a second that I am anything other than totally and utterly obsessed with her.

7

OLIVIA

I SLIDE DOWN HIS BODY, sinking to my knees in front of him, and lift my gaze to meet his as I undo his pants. I can already tell just from the touch I've stolen that he has the most beautiful cock, and I know that I want to meet it face to face, so to speak.

"Fuck," he groans as I slide my hand beneath his boxers and pull out his erection.

I gasp as soon as I see it – so long and so thick around the middle that I have a hard time fitting my hand around it. I don't think that I have ever seen a cock this impressive in person before – and knowing that the person attached to it is a real man, who knows what he wants and how to get it is all the better.

"Mmm," I moan as I lean forward to swirl my

tongue around his head. I can already taste the pre-cum leaking from his cock, and I know that he must have been trying to contain this since the moment that he saw me out on that porch, touching myself. I knew that there had been someone watching me, and the thought of it being him – the thought of this beautiful cock getting hard over me, that is everything that I need right now.

"Think I need to get a better feel for the dimensions," I flirt with him playfully as I wrap both hands around his length and begin to stroke him up and down. "If I'm really going to capture it the way that you want."

I slip my lips over his head and inch them down, until his whole length is engulfed in either my mouth or my hands – I can feel his tension, how much he wants me, and I slide one hand to his thigh to rake my nails down it playfully. He shivers. I know it has nothing to do with the storm outside, and everything to do with the way his beautiful dick feels in my mouth right now.

"Fuck, that feels good," he groans, and I look up at him again – he reaches down to cup my head in his hand, guiding me a little further down. I imagine that he's never been a man who has had to work hard to get his dick sucked, and it thrills me to see the way that he is looking at me right now, as though I am the most tempting morsel that has ever fallen onto his plate.

I take my time to work as much of him into my mouth as I can manage, until I feel his head pressing at the back of my throat. I can't take my eyes off of him, can't stop looking at him as he responds to me, to what I am doing to him. This is everything that I have been waiting for, everything that I have been wanting, even before I knew it – his hands on me, showing me how to pleasure him the way he likes best.

He pushes his hips forward a couple of inches, testing out just how much of him I can take, and I close my eyes and move my other hand to his thigh so that he can fuck my mouth properly. I want to be used by him. I want to be taken by him. I want to do everything that he needs to make him come. Even if this is the only time that I am ever going to be with him, I want to make sure that he remembers every single second of it.

He slides his cock in and out of my mouth in shallow thrusts, making sure not to push in too deep and make me gag. I wrap my hands around his muscular thighs and let him enjoy all that I am giving.

I can't wait to feel this cock in my pussy – I know that he's going to make me feel incredible, I can just tell from how careful he is with me on my knees in front of him.

I pull back to catch my breath, a string of saliva still attaching my lips to the tip of his cock, and he grasps my chin and pulls me to my feet so that he can look me in the eyes. Something about how powerful he is really hits me – this man can do anything that he wants to me, and I know that I would enjoy each and every moment of it. Because any second that he is gifting me his time is one that I am going to treasure.

"Bedroom," he tells me as he plants his lips on my neck, slides his mouth over my throat, makes sure to bare his teeth against my skin. I swear, I melt right into him, unable to think about anything other than doing just what he tells me. Gone is that gentleman who came here today. And in his place is a man who's willing to do anything that it takes to get what he needs from me.

8

GAGE

I TOSS her down onto the bed and pounce on top of her, my cock so hard as it grinds against her thigh that I wonder how I am going to make it another moment without just shoving myself inside of her and fucking her until she's crying out my name.

The way she just got down on her knees and blew me like that – God, it was fucking hot. I don't have much time to date, what with running the business and all, and maybe it's just because it's been a long time since I've been with anyone, but I feel this connection with her that I've never had with a single person in my life.

She wraps her legs around me and pulls me down on top of her, kissing me hard, our tongues coming together like we are both starved for one another. She is only wearing some shorts and a light tee, and I can feel her hard nipples pressing against my chest through it.

I pull it off her body and toss it aside, diving down to suck and nibble on her nipples – she groans and holds my head in place, and I savor the sweet taste of her pink breast in my mouth.

"I've been thinking about this since I saw you out there, playing with yourself," I murmur to her. "You know how fucking hot you were?"

"I hoped that you were watching," she gasps as I slide up to kiss her again. "I was thinking of you the entire time."

"Want me to show you what it's really like?" I ask as I push my hand down her panties, find her clit. She closes her eyes, her body squirming with pleasure beneath mine.

"Tell me what you want," I order her. I want to hear it out of her mouth. That she wants me as much as I want her.

"I want you to play with my pussy," she gasps to me, finally, and it's all the excuse I need to guide my fingers down to her dripping-wet slit and push them inside for the first time.

Fuck, she's tight. I know that she's going to feel even better wrapped around my cock, but right now, I just want to watch her come all over my hand, the same way that she did when she was playing with herself. She pushes her hips up to meet me, giving me all the access that I need, and I slide an arm around her waist to support her as I fuck her sweet little pussy with my hand.

"Oh my God," she gasps, and her eyes practically roll back into her head. I push my fingers all the way inside of her, hold them there, moving them slowly side to side, so that she can feel every part of them inside of her.

"Tell me how good it feels," I order her.

"It feels fucking incredible," she moans, and she manages to grab me again, this time pulling my head down to hers so that she can kiss me once more. I move my fingers inside of her again, and then slide them up to play with her clit. I want her to feel everything that she can, all the pleasure that's possible for this hot little body of hers to experience.

It doesn't take long till I feel her starting to tense underneath me, and I know that she must be getting close to coming. She grasps my shoulder tight, humping my hand. And finally, I feel her pussy contract around my fingers, tightening for a long moment before she crashes back onto the bed and lets out a gasp of relief.

"Oh," she moans, and I pull my fingers out of her, push them past her lips – like the petals of the flower, they open at once to take me, and she swirls her tongue around my fingers and draws me in like she has been waiting for me all this time.

"I need you to fuck me," she begs, her voice throaty, catching at the edges. "Please, Gage..."

As soon as she murmurs that to me, I know that I can't hold back. I push her legs apart, pull off her panties, and take my cock into my hand, guiding it against her soaking-wet slit and pushing inside of her in one swift motion.

The sound she makes as I push inside her for the first time is unlike anything I have ever heard before. Her body rises from the bed for a moment as she moves against me, taking me in as deep as I can go. Her pussy is stretched wide around my cock, and I sit back on the bed, taking a moment to look at her gorgeous cunt opening to fit my hard-on. And then, I move on top of her, wrap my arms around her, and begin to fuck her properly.

It's like our bodies have been made to go together like this. As she lifts her hips to let me in even deeper, I drive myself all the way up to the hilt inside her pussy, over and over again, the only sound in the room that of our flesh coming together and the sharp breaths she lets out every time I slide into her again. I can't take my eyes off her face – she has the same expression that she did when she was coming all over her hand before, her eyes glazed with want as though nothing matters but the pleasure that's blooming between her legs.

"Fuck, fuck, fuck," she groans, and she presses her head against my shoulder. I can tell that she is getting close again, and the thought of her coming is enough to make my balls tingle. I know that I am not far from orgasm myself, and I want to bottom out deep inside of her. I slam myself into her again, again, again, until finally...

When I feel my cock twitch inside of her, it seems to be all that she needs to take herself over the edge. She tips her head back and lets out a moan so long and so loud that I am sure everyone else in the houses around us will hear it. I pull her close, our bodies flat against one another, and feel her pussy clench around my cock, over and over again, her relief and her release passing from her body to mine and back again as the pleasure takes control of us both.

I hold myself inside of her for a long while before I pull out, but finally, I withdraw from her once more, and I roll down onto the bed beside her. She laughs, rolls over too, and plants her hand against my chest. My heart is beating so fast I am certain that she must be able to feel it through my skin.

"Well, hey, neighbor," she greets me playfully, as though we're just seeing each other for the first time. And honestly? Honestly, I feel like we are. And I can't wait to find out what we have in store for each other next.

9

OLIVIA

When I wake the next morning, it's to the sound of rain pattering on the windows – and the soft, slow breath of the man who is sleeping in bed next to me.

I roll over to face him, and smile. He stayed the night. Not that it would have mattered much if he had decided to go home or anything, since he's so close by, but still – it's been a long time since I last woke up beside another person, and the sight of his handsome, angular face on the pillow beside me is everything I need right now.

As though sensing my eyes on him, he slowly opens his own, and grins at me when he sees me staring. He reaches for me under the covers, and pulls me against him into a warm embrace.

"Well, hey," he murmurs throatily.

"Didn't expect you to stay the night," I remark, and he cocks an eyebrow at me.

"You expected me to dump you before you even woke up?"

"Something like that," I confess, and he laughs, plants a kiss on my cheek.

"You know, it's a good thing you're so damn cute," he tells me. "Otherwise I might be insulted that you really thought I would just dump you after last night. You want some breakfast?"

"That would be lovely," I reply, feeling a little shy all of a sudden. Which I know is crazy, after everything that we did last night, but I can't help it. Something about this guy, about his confidence, about the certainty in the way he carries himself, makes me feel fluttery inside in the best way possible.

He heads downstairs, and I toss on a pair of panties and a shirt and follow him. He seems to know his way around this place, and doesn't wait around. He makes us something to eat – eggs and bacon, some toast and some juice.

"I thought guys like you didn't need to learn how to cook," I remark as he hands me a plate to take out onto the back porch since the rain has stopped.

"We don't need to, we choose to," he replies, offering me a warm smile as he joins me. There is a small table with a couple of chairs outside, and the sun that is clearing the clouds above us is gorgeous and welcoming.

"Good to know," I tell him. I feel giddy, like I have no idea how to keep the smile off of my face right now. There's just something so... so thrilling about him. Something that makes it hard for my dumb ass to think straight.

"Can I ask you something?" he wonders aloud, and I nod.

"Of course."

"Did you want me to see you yesterday so I would come here?"

I grin at him, and nod again. There's no point denying the truth.

"I thought you were sexy when I first saw you, I just didn't really know how to say it," I confess. "So I thought... well, it got the message across, right?"

"It sure did," he agrees, and he slides his hand over mine on the table. I feel dizzy. Something as simple as his touch is enough to make me feel like I am going to swoon.

"How long are you going to be here?" he asks me softly.

"The whole summer, probably," I reply. "At least until Leanne gets home."

A smile spreads across his lips and I can tell that it's the answer he was hoping for.

"I hope you don't mind, but I intend to spend as much time as possible with you while you're here," he murmurs, and he takes my hand and brings it to his lips, planting a kiss against it softly. The warm touch of his lips is so damn romantic that I can't help but smile.

"I think that sounds just perfect," I agree, and he reaches over to brush a loose strand of hair back from my face. Where the hell did he learn to be so perfect, so romantic, so sweet? I have questions. At least now I know he is in no rush to get away from me, and I am going to have the time to find out the answers to those questions. Which is something that I intend to do.

"Still want me to paint a portrait for you?" I remind him playfully, and he laughs.

"I'm not sure about that," he replies. "But I'd like to see some more of your work."

"Why, you thinking of buying?"

"My business partner and I are art dealers," he remarks. "So maybe we can get some of your work in front of the right people."

My jaw drops. I can't believe what I'm hearing.

"You're serious?"

"Totally."

"That would be amazing!" I exclaim, and I practically leap out of my seat to jump into his lap. He laughs and slides his arms around my waist, looking up at me as though he can hardly believe that I am really here with him right now.

"Perfect," he murmurs, and he leans in to kiss me again. I close my eyes and let my lips find his once more, and wonder how the hell I managed to find someone this perfect for me – someone who seems to have all the pieces that I've been looking for, sitting right here beside me. I smile into the kiss, unable to hide how much I want him right now, and feel a warmth stirring in the bottom of my belly. Because I know that this is real. Whatever it is – it's real. And I'm not going to let it slip through my fingers.

EPILOGUE
GAGE

"Are you sure that's everything?" I ask her as she brings the last of her art stuff out of the house and plants it in the back of her car. She puts her hands on her hips, surveys everything, and then nods.

"I think it is," she replies, and she manages a smile. Even though I know that the last thing she wants to do is grin right now.

It's the end of the summer, and Olivia is headed to her roommate filledf apartment. Leanne will be back in town later today, and Olivia promised to make herself scarce by the time she rolled up. I have been helping her pack up her stuff all day, and trying to hold in the one question that I want to ask her. I know that she plans to go. But I don't want to let her leave.

"I can't believe I have to go back to living with my roommates again," she sighs, and I wrap my arms around her. Cuddling her comes so natural to me these days; we've spent so many nights wrapped up in each other that it just comes easy to me now.

"I know, I'm going to miss you so much," I reply. We agreed that this little fling of ours would last the summer, but now I am facing the reality of her leaving, and that is the last thing I want. Maybe I need to be honest – maybe I need to come clean. Tell her what's been on my mind.

"Something bothering you?" she asks me, pulling back to look at me. She has gotten to know me so well that she can already tell when something is on my mind. I take a deep breath, and nod. I know I shouldn't be nervous. I am sure she is going to say yes.

"Something is, actually," I admit. "I – I don't want you to go, Olivia."

"What are you talking about?" she asks.

"I want you to stay here, with me," I continue. All the things that I have been considering inside my head, they are starting to become clear to me.

"You can move into my place, I have room for you to have a whole studio of your own, finish art school," I explain. "You can paint, you don't have to worry about being disturbed – you can have the whole place to yourself when I'm away on business, if that's what you need. Just... don't go back to your roommates."

She stares at me for a moment. And I stare back at her, at this woman who I have come to love. And the next words spill out of my mouth before I can stop them. I know that they're right. And I know that I can't let her leave this place until she's heard them from me.

"Marry me, Olivia."

Her lips parted in surprise – the way I had seen them do so many times before I kissed her, before I pulled her close, before I told her that her paintings were going to be in one of the biggest galleries in New York, where they belong. I love that look, that moment of anticipation before she works out what she is going to tell me. But this time, I am sure that I know what she is going to say before she manages to get the words out.

"Yes!" she exclaims, and she practically launches herself into my arms. "Yes, of course I'll marry you," she cries into my ear.

I catch her and hold her tight, unable to keep the smile off my face. When I saw that gorgeous woman pulling up in that junker car all those weeks ago, the last thing I expected was to be begging her not to get in it again and go. But I've ended up right where I need to be – with this woman in my arms, with her in my life, with the two of us together.

And I wouldn't have it any other way.

Harrison

I RUN a hand over my beard as I look down at the
wild mint growing beside my cabin. Pressing a

green leaf between my thumb and forefinger, I think about the next chapter I'm working on for my survival guide -- medicinal herbs found in the Alaskan wild. Mint like this can help with pain and inflammation. This tiny green leaf can do so much.

But I'm not naive enough to think it can help with the pain in my heart.

Nothing can.

Still, I hold onto this crazy hope that maybe, just maybe my mother was right. Maybe love can cure all ailments.

It's why I ordered a bride.

I pick a handful of the mint and walk toward my cabin, feeling that never-ending phantom pain in my prosthetic leg.

As I push open the door to my cabin, my cell phone on the counter begins to ring. Setting down the mint, I answer it.

"Harrison?" my twin brother, Sullivan, asks.

"Who else would be answering?" I retort snarkily as I fill a jar with water and place the freshly picked stalks in it, then grab myself a beer from the fridge and go outside to my back porch. It's my favorite place on this entire stretch of land. Facing a rushing river, with big pine trees reaching to the sky, thickets of wild blackberry brambles where deer graze undisturbed--it's paradise.

"You left a message? Something about Mom's wedding ring?"

I clear my throat. "Uh, yeah. Just wanted to make sure you were okay with me using it. I know we never really discussed it. I have her things, though, and--"

Sully cuts me off. "You're asking someone to marry you?"

I frown. "Do you care?"

"You're my twin fucking brother, Harry. Of course, I care."

"I know you have your own life in Anchorage. I just didn't think you'd really..."

"What?" Irritation is laced through his single word.

"You're not exactly sentimental, Sully."

"And you are? The last thing you told me was that you were going off the grid for good. Now you call asking if it's okay to give someone Mom's diamond ring? You see where I might be a little confused?"

I rake a hand through my hair. "I know."

"Who is she?" Sully asks.

"Does it make a difference?"

"God, Harry. Could you try and go easy on

me? I know I'm not the war vet, but hell, I'm still your brother. You're my only family."

"Look, nevermind," I say, picking up my beer and taking a swig. "I don't need to use Mom's ring."

The call goes quiet and for a moment I think he might have hung up.

Then he speaks. "You sure you're okay, man? I know things are hard sometimes, after everything you've been through. Maybe you should talk to someone?"

I groan into my beer. "Sul, all I did for a year after I got home was talk to someone. I'm fine now. I'm doing what I want, where I want."

"And you want to get engaged? Where did you even meet her? Don't you live in the middle of bum-fuck, Nowhereland?"

I snort, trying to push down the truth. I know he'll judge me for it. Sullivan has never had a hard time dating women. Or, more correctly, sleeping with them.

Me?

Well. Let's just say I haven't had much experience. Make that *any experience*.

And now with my war injury, I can't see myself getting on Tinder and looking for a hookup. Besides, there isn't a woman within fifty miles of this cabin.

"Dude, Harrison, are you even listening?" he asks.

"Sorry, what?" I was lost in my fucking insecurities.

"I was asking who this girl is?"

"Honestly? Uh, I don't know, man."

He snorts. "You don't know?"

"Yeah," I say, refusing to feel judged. "I ordered a bride."

"You what?"

"You heard me, Sul. I ordered a bride. She's coming next week. And I need to give her a ring."

"That's so fucking weird," he says, laughing. "Do you even know what she looks like?"

"I'm gonna hang up now," I tell him. I have no interest in Sullivan's condescension.

"It's just, Harrison, you're a fucking Green Beret. A Special Ops war hero. You don't need to buy a wife."

Easy for him to say. He didn't lose his leg in Afghanistan. He didn't go through the pain of watching his friends die in a war zone. He didn't have to fucking piece together a life after losing so damn much.

Not to mention, he's not a virgin.

I am.

I can't fucking go meet a girl and try to act normal. Nothing about me is normal, especially, not after the shit I've seen. I'm a changed man and there is no going back.

"I want to do this, Sullivan," I tell him plainly. "I don't expect you to understand." We may be twins, but we're so goddamn different.

"Can I at least come to the wedding?" he asks, still cracking up.

"No."

"Fuck, Harrison. You know, for a hero, you're a pretty big asshole."

"Look, we're going to the courthouse after I pick her up. It's not gonna be a thing. It's all pretty straightforward."

"You have any idea what you're getting into, brother? Women like weddings. White dresses. Flowers. Cake. The whole nine yards."

I contemplate his words. Fuck. All that stuff hasn't been on my radar. I thought I was being prepared by finding her a ring.

"You think?" I ask apprehensively. To be honest, I've mostly been worried about our wedding night. I'm a fucking twenty-seven-year-old virgin.

"Yeah. Get some flowers for the wedding at the very least, and some sort of cake. Some rose petals on the bed? Women like that shit, I'm telling you."

"And the ring?"

"You sure she's gonna stick around after she sees where you live?"

I clench my jaw, looking around my cabin. It's small, but it's modern, and everything in it is less than a year old. "I hope so."

"Go with your gut, then. It's never served you wrong before."

I laugh wryly. "Let's hope you're right."

"Worse case scenario, she's just a good lay."

"Hey," I say sharply. "Don't talk about my bride like that."

He laughs. "Damn, man, you haven't even met her and you're already protective. Just make sure you don't scare her away; you aren't exactly an open book."

"Don't worry," I tell him. "The agency did a screening. They are sending the right woman for me."

"How much did she cost?" Sully asks.

Now it's my turn to laugh. "Why? You considering using some of your trust fund to buy a wife?"

He laughs. "Nah, I get plenty of pussy as it is. Don't need to settle down."

I hang up with my brother, thinking we couldn't be more different.

I just hope the woman running the agency, Isabella, found the right woman for me because

Sullivan is right about one thing: I've never opened up with a woman before.

And now, I'll have no choice.

I may be a wounded warrior, but I'm also a mountain man.

When it comes to commitment, I'm going all in.

Let's hope this bride who's coming can handle me.

Ready to read the rest of this yummy modern mail-order bride romance?
Download The Mountain Man's Cure at your favorite retailer!

ABOUT THE AUTHOR

Frankie Love writes filthy-sweet stories about
bad boys and mountain men.
Frankie is ridiculously in love with her own
bearded hottie, believes in love-at-first-sight, and
happily-ever-afters. She also believes in the
power of a quickie.

Find Frankie here:
www.frankielove.net
frankieloveromance@gmail.com